MO
and His Friends

MARY POPE OSBORNE

PICTURES BY

DyAnne DiSalvo-Ryan

DIAL BOOKS FOR YOUNG READERS
NEW YORK

Dial easy-to-read

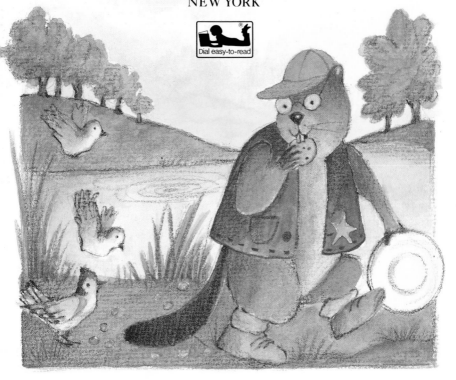

For Ken Whelan, the real Mo
—M.P.O.

For Vanessa and Michael Jo
—D.D.

Published by Dial Books for Young Readers
A Division of Penguin Books USA Inc.
375 Hudson Street
New York, New York 10014

Text copyright © 1989 by Mary Pope Osborne
Pictures copyright © 1989 by DyAnne DiSalvo-Ryan
All rights reserved
Printed in Hong Kong by South China Printing Company (1988) Limited

The Dial Easy-to-Read logo is a registered trademark of
Dial Books for Young Readers,
a division of Penguin Books USA Inc.,
® TM 1,162,718.

Library of Congress Cataloging in Publication Data
Osborne, Mary Pope. Mo and his friends / by Mary Pope Osborne;
pictures by DyAnne DiSalvo-Ryan.
p. cm.
Summary: Brief stories feature Sheriff Mo and his animal friends.
[1. Friendship—Fiction. 2. Animals—Fiction.]
I. DiSalvo-Ryan, DyAnne, ill. II. Title.
PZ7.081167Mm 1989 [E]—dc19 87-15655 CIP AC
E

First Hardcover Printing 1989
ISBN 0-8037-0504-2 (tr.) ISBN 0-8037-0505-0 (lib. bdg.)
1 3 5 7 9 10 8 6 4 2

First Trade Paperback Printing 1991
ISBN 0-8037-0924-2 (pb.)
1 3 5 7 9 10 8 6 4 2

The full-color artwork was produced using pencil, colored pencil,
and watercolor washes. It was then scanner-separated and reproduced
as red, blue, yellow, and black halftones.

Reading Level 2.1

Contents

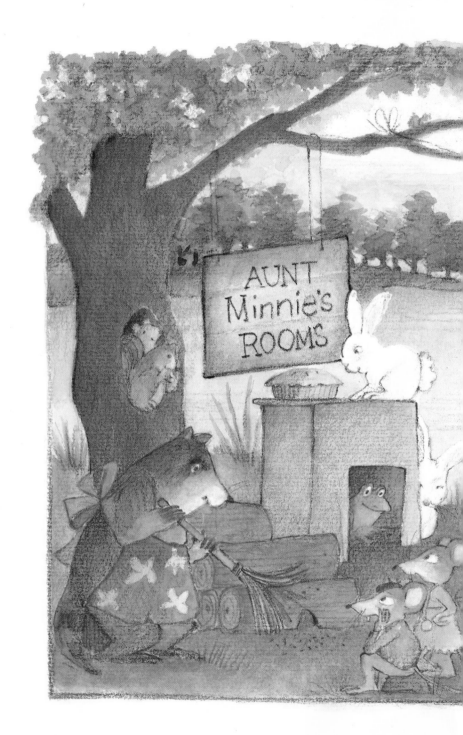

AUNT MINNIE TAKES A BREAK

Aunt Minnie worked very hard

in her boardinghouse

beside Smith Pond.

She cooked and swept.

She washed clothes

and fixed broken steps.

"Aunt Minnie needs a break,"
Peewee said.

"She certainly does!" said Pearl.

"Let's give her a vacation."

"Good idea," said Peewee.

So Pearl and Peewee had a bake sale
and a car wash to raise money
for Aunt Minnie's vacation.

Then they had a party
for Aunt Minnie.
"Aunt Minnie, here's fifty dollars!"
Pearl said.
"For a vacation in Florida!"

Aunt Minnie clapped her hands.
"You are so nice to do this!" she said.

Chicken Lucille helped Aunt Minnie

pack for her trip.

Then Peewee bought her a bus ticket.

The night before Aunt Minnie left,

Sheriff Mo heard a knock on his door.

"Aunt Minnie! Come in!

Sit down!" he said. "How are you?"

"Oh, Sheriff," Aunt Minnie said.

"I don't want to go away!"

She burst into a flood of tears.

"I'll be just miserable

without all my friends."

"Oh, I see, I see," said Mo,

patting her on the back.

"Well, don't worry, Aunt Minnie.

I'll think of something."

The next morning everyone took
Aunt Minnie to the bus station.
"Where's Sheriff Mo?" asked Aunt Minnie.
"He said he would meet us here,"
said Chicken Lucille.

Just then the bus pulled up.

"Oh, dear, oh, dear," said Aunt Minnie.

"We must wait for the sheriff!"

"We'll tell Mo you said good-bye,"

said Pearl. "It's time to go now."

Just then the door to the bus opened.

"All aboard!" shouted Sheriff Mo.

Mo was the bus driver!

"We are all going on a trip!" he said.

"Together!"

Then Mo drove everyone to the beach.

For three days they had a great time.

Peewee took pictures

as they built sandcastles,

and Sheriff Mo read

under a striped umbrella.

Then they all came back home,
sunburned and happy.
And Aunt Minnie stayed up all night
sweeping sand out of the bus.

THE QUEEN BY THE POND

One day Pearl and Peewee spied
a strange creature
strolling around Smith Pond.
She appeared to be a queen.

She wore a gold crown on her head
and a long purple cape.
And she had on a white mask
and waved a large flowered fan.
"*Who* is that?" said Peewee.
"Oh, dear! I don't know!" said Pearl.

The two of them ran to Sheriff Mo's.

"Hurry, Sheriff!" they cried.

"A strange creature who looks like
a queen is walking around the pond!"

"Goodness," said Mo.

And he rushed to the pond
with Pearl and Peewee.

Now many other animals were watching the queen in the white mask strolling about, waving her fan.

"Excuse me, madame," said Mo.

"But what are you doing here?"

"Enjoying your lovely sun, Sheriff," said the queen in a high voice.

"Who are you?" asked Mo.

"You may call me Queen Blanche," the queen said sweetly.

"Ah!" said Mo.

He recognized a familiar voice.

"I have an idea, madame," he said.

Everyone watched as Mo got
some boards and a hammer and nails,
and made a little platform.
Then he put up a curtain.

"From now on everyone can come here to see plays!" he said.

"What plays?" asked Pearl.

"Plays starring Chicken Lucille!" Mo said.

Later Chicken Lucille said to Mo,
"My dream of being an actress
has finally come true, thanks to you."
"You deserve it, Lucille," said Mo
as everyone applauded.

PEEWEE'S SURPRISE

Early one autumn morning

Chicken Lucille, Aunt Minnie, and Mo

knocked on Peewee's door.

"I'm coming," called Peewee.

He took a large sack from his closet.

Then he left the house with
Aunt Minnie, Mo, and Chicken Lucille.
They tramped into the woods
and picked nuts and acorns
off the ground.

They picked apples
off the apple trees
and berries off the berry bushes
and put them into Peewee's sack.

Then they walked beside a stream.

And near the water

Aunt Minnie found a blue stone.

Chicken Lucille found a pink stone.

They put them both in Peewee's sack.

Then Peewee climbed a maple tree
and pulled red leaves
off the branches.

And Mo picked purple clover,
wild daisies, and buttercups.
They put them all in Peewee's sack.

Then Sheriff Mo, Aunt Minnie,
Chicken Lucille, and Peewee
went to Pearl's house.

Inside, Pearl was reading a book.

The doorbell rang,

but when she opened the door,

no one was there.

"Who rang?" she shouted.

"What's this old sack doing here?"
Pearl reached into the sack
and pulled out the apples
and nuts and berries.

"Oh, boy, look at these!"

she said to herself.

"I can make pies!"

Then Pearl pulled out

the pink and blue stones

and the red leaves.

"Oh, swell! Look at these!"

she said to herself.

Then Pearl reached further

into the sack—

and she screamed, "Eek!"

Peewee jumped out of the sack.

He had purple clover all over him.

The others came out of the bushes.

"Here we are!" shouted Peewee.

"All your favorite things!

Happy birthday, sweetheart!"

GHOSTS

Often when it snowed in the winter,

Mo and his friends

went to Aunt Minnie's.

They sat by the fire
and played cards.
They drank hot chocolate
and told stories to each other.

One night Peewee told

a very scary story

about a ghost.

When he finished, the animals heard

a creaking noise in the hall.

"Oh, dear! A ghost!"

cried Aunt Minnie.

40

"No, no, Aunt Minnie," said Sheriff Mo.

"Ghosts aren't real.

It's only the old wood singing a song."

Suddenly the curtain moved
and a strange sound
came from the window.
"Eek!" cried Pearl. "A ghost!"
"No, no, Pearl," said Mo.
"Ghosts aren't real.
It's only the wind saying hello."

Then scratching sounds

came from the wall.

"Sheriff!" cried Peewee.

"It's a ghost!"

"No, no, Peewee," said Mo.

"It's only a little mouse in the wall

trying to keep warm."

"Oh, Sheriff!" cried Chicken Lucille.

"I hear breathing sounds!

It's a ghost!"

"Lucille, Lucille, don't fret,"

said Mo. "It's only the daylight

sleeping and dreaming."

All the animals were very quiet

as they listened to the sounds

of the wood and the north wind

and the mouse and the daylight.

Suddenly a picture fell off the wall behind Sheriff Mo.

Mo leaped out of his chair.

"A *ghost!*"

"Sheriff, Sheriff, it's only
a picture falling!" the animals cried.
"Goodness, goodness!" said Mo,
holding his heart.

All the animals laughed at Mo.

The sheriff himself laughed hardest.

"Let's toast good friends!" he said.

"Hear, hear!" everyone cheered.